All's Well That Ends Well

Sweet Cherry
Publishing

Published by Sweet Cherry Publishing Limited
Unit E, Vulcan Business Complex,
Vulcan Road,
Leicester, LE5 3EB,
United Kingdom

First published in the USA in 2013
ISBN: 978-1-78226-066-0

©Macaw Books

Title: All's Well That Ends Well
North American Edition

All rights reserved. No part of this publication may be
reproduced or utilized in any form or by any means, electronic
or mechanical, including photocopying, recording, or using
any information storage and retrieval system, without prior
permission in writing from the publisher.

Text & Illustration by Macaw Books 2013

www.sweetcherrypublishing.com

Printed and bound by Wai Man Book Binding (China) Ltd. Kowloon, H.K.

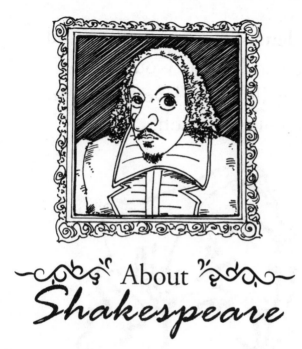

~~ About ~~ *Shakespeare*

William Shakespeare, regarded as the greatest writer in the English language, was born in Stratford-upon-Avon in Warwickshire, England (around April 23, 1564). He was the third of eight children born to John and Mary Shakespeare.

Shakespeare was a poet, playwright, and dramatist. He is often known as England's national poet and the "Bard of Avon." Thirty-eight plays, 154 sonnets, two long narrative poems, and several other poems are attributed to him. Shakespeare's plays have been translated into every major existent language and are performed more often than those of any other playwright.

Helena: She is an orphan and the ward of the Countess of Rousillon. She loves Bertram, the countess's son.

Bertram: A handsome young man and a skilled soldier. He is the countess's son. He unwillingly marries Helena before abandoning her.

Diana: She is a young woman whom Bertram wants to make his mistress. She helps Helena get her husband back.

King of France: The King of France likes Helena and is upset about Bertram's behavior toward her.

All's Well That Ends Well

Bertram had been named the Count of Rousillon a short while ago after his father died, leaving him the title and the estate. The King of France and Bertram's father were very close friends, and so the moment the king learned of his friend's death, he sent for Bertram to offer him his special favor and to bring him under his protection.

Lafeu, an old minister in the French court, came to inform Bertram of the king's orders. Since the king was the absolute monarch in France at that time, any order he gave had to be adhered to, irrespective of

a person's rank or state. So Bertram knew that he would have to go back with Lafeu immediately. His mother, with whom he was living at the time, was sad to see her son go away so soon. First she had lost her husband, and now her son.

But Lafeu reassured her that the king was very kind and wanted to take young Bertram under his wing after the death of his father. He also told her that the king was suffering from a very serious malady for which there seemed to be no cure. Bertram's mother mentioned Helena, a young girl who lived with her, and her late father. She explained

that Gerard de Narbon had
been a great physician, able
to cure almost any disease. At
the time of his death, he had
wished that his only daughter,
Helena, should come to stay with
Bertram's mother, and Helena
had lived with her ever since. She
also told him how Helena had

inherited all her father's virtues and his excellent disposition.

While Bertram's mother spoke of the great Gerard de Narbon, Helena, who was close by, started weeping.

Soon, Bertram bade his mother good-bye. The Countess asked Lafeu to take good care of her son, for he was still an

unseasoned courtier. Before leaving, Bertram spoke to Helena, asking her to take good care of his mother.

While it was true that Helena had been very fond of her late father, her tears were for another reason entirely. She had long been in love with Bertram, and now that he was going away, she could no longer conceal her sadness. But she also knew how different they both were. While Bertram was the Count of Rousillon, Helena was just the daughter of a humble physician. Therefore, she considered herself lucky to be the servant of the house and looked upon Bertram as her master.

Helena's father, the great physician Gerard de Narbon, had left her some prescriptions of rare virtue, which he had acquired through his long study and experience in medicine. These remedies that he had created could not fail under any circumstances. As she went through them once again during Bertram's absence, she found an antidote for the illness the king had contracted.

Helena made a secret pact
with herself that she would
go to Paris and cure the king
of his disease. But then more
pragmatic thoughts crossed her
mind; after all, had the king's
own physicians not told him
that his illness was incurable?
Why, then, would he listen to

the advice of a young girl? But she knew that her father's revered cures were perhaps her only chance to one day become the wife of the Count of Rousillon.

While Helena was pondering the matter and speaking her thoughts out loud,

a steward who worked with her overheard what she said. He immediately went to Bertram's mother and told her what he had heard. But instead of being angry with Helena, Bertram's mother just smiled, remembering her own youthful days.

Helena entered the room, unaware that the lady of the house knew all about her feelings. Bertram's mother spoke to her very

kindly and told her how she
felt like a mother to her, but
Helena just turned pale at the
words and realized her love for
Bertram was no longer a secret.

She expressed how fortunate she was to have such a kind mistress, but Bertram's mother kept declaring her motherly feelings toward Helena. Finally, the

young girl blurted out, "Pardon me, madam, but you are not my mother; the Count of Rousillon cannot be my brother, nor I your daughter." Only then did the noble Count-mother say, "But you can be my daughter-in-law. Don't you want it to be this way?"

Helena did not know
what to say. When she finally
confessed, Bertram's mother
asked her if she wanted to go to
Paris to be with Bertram. Helena
merely replied that it was not just
Bertram she had been thinking
of in connection with her visit to
Paris. She mentioned the king's
illness and how she knew of a

remedy that had belonged to her
father, which would surely cure
the ailing monarch. The Count-
mother knew that this would
perhaps be the finest moment for
Gerard de Narbon's daughter to
announce herself to the world,

so she immediately gave her leave to head for Paris, along with enough money and attendants to accompany her.

Once she reached
Paris, Helena got in
touch with the kind
old Lafeu and told him
of the remedy that
would surely cure the
king. However, it was
not easy for her to be
seen by the monarch.
After all, why would
the king trust a young
girl's medicines, when
all the physicians in
the country had failed?
But Helena informed
him that she was
indeed the daughter
of the great Gerard de
Narbon, someone the

king had always held in high
regard, so the king decided to go
ahead with the treatment. But
before Helena could administer
the medicine, the king made a
deal with her—if the medicine
did not cure him in two days'

time, then Helena would pay for it with her life; however, if he were to recover, then she had the right to choose a husband from all the men present in the whole of France.

Helena had indeed been right about her father's medicinal powers, for before the two days had passed, the king was back on his feet. He claimed that he had never felt as well as he did now. He agreed that he had lost the wager with Helena and asked all the noblemen in his

33

court to assemble before them
one fine day. Helena went round
and finally spotted Bertram.
She informed the king of her
choice and the king was only too
happy with it. But Bertram was
not amused and showed clear
disdain toward the proceedings,

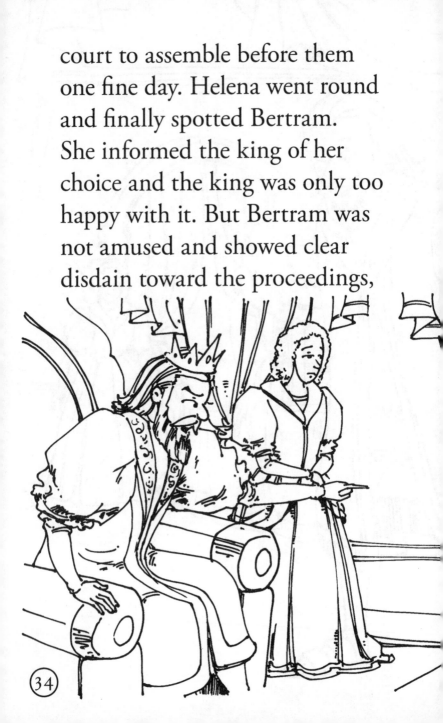

refusing to marry the daughter of a poor physician and someone who worked in his own house.

The king was livid about Bertram's behavior, since Helena's choice had been the result of a royal wager and Bertram was clearly being disrespectful toward him. So he forced the marriage and very soon, Bertram and Helena were married. But it was a sad marriage, since Bertram did not love Helena at all.

As soon as the marriage was concluded, Bertram asked the king for leave of absence. Before leaving, Bertram told Helena to go back to his mother and take good care of her. He informed her that this sudden marriage had shaken him considerably and he wanted to be by himself. Helena only replied that as his most obedient servant, she would continue to do as he wished, but Bertram was already gone.

Helena went back to
the Count-mother with
a heavy heart. She had
met both her objectives in
traveling to France—having
cured the king's incurable
disease and also marrying
the man of her dreams—
yet she had brought back
with her no joy. What
hurt her the most was the
letter she received from
Bertram when she reached
Rousillon, telling her that
only if she could remove
the ring from his finger,
which he would never
remove on his own, could
she call him her husband.

The Count-mother tried
her best to console her daughter-
in-law, but Helena's broken
heart could find no solace in
her arms. She kept staring at a
particular phrase in the letter,
which said, "Till I have no
wife, I have nothing in France."
Neither Helena nor her mother-

in-law could believe the words
that Bertram had put together
in this letter to his wife.

The next morning, when the
Count-mother awoke, Helena
was nowhere to be found. Finally,
one of the servants brought her
a letter from Helena, which
said that the poor girl was so

heartbroken following Bertram's
actions that she had decided
to leave Rousillon and go on a
pilgrimage to the shrine of St.
Jacques le Grand. She begged her
mother-in-law's forgiveness and

asked her to inform her son that the wife he so detested had gone away, so he could return home.

Meanwhile, Bertram had left France for the Italian city of Florence, where he had become an officer in the duke's army. After fighting many valiant wars, he had distinguished himself through his brave actions. One day, Bertram received a letter from his mother informing him that his wife had left forever, so he decided to return home. Little did he know that destiny had recently brought a young pilgrim to Florence, none other than Helena.

The shrine of St. Jacques le Grand, the place to which Helena was going, was a short distance from Florence. Once Helena reached the beautiful city, she decided to go to a kind widow who offered lodgings to female pilgrims and looked after them during their

stay in Florence. The widow very
kindly welcomed Helena and
offered to show her the sights
around the city. She mentioned
that she would also take her to
see the duke's army, and she
could perhaps even meet a fellow

countryman serving in the army, the Count of Rousillon.

Helena did not need to be asked twice and got ready to visit the army immediately. When they saw Bertram from a distance, the widow casually remarked, "Is he not handsome?" and Helena simply said in return, "I like him well." The lady then went on to tell Helena about Bertram's past, and how he had run away to

Florence to escape from his wife. As the lady continued her story, Helena's heart sank. The widow told her about Bertram's love for a woman called Diana, her own daughter. He would try to meet her after the rest of the family had retired for the night, singing love songs in praise of her beauty. But Diana knew that Bertram was a married man and therefore did not reciprocate his feelings of love. Helena also learned from her hostess that Bertram was going to leave Florence forever the next morning.

Helena immediately came up with a plan to bring back her truant husband. She made a full confession to the widow that she was the wife of the Count, and the old widow at once agreed to help her in any way possible to

make Bertram fall in love with
her. So Diana, her daughter, sent
a message to Bertram saying that
she would like to see him one last
time before he left for France.

Helena had another
message sent to Bertram stating

that she had died during the
pilgrimage, so that he would
not suspect anything later that
night. When Bertram stole into
Diana's chambers, he found the
woman of his dreams waiting
for him. Little did he know that
the woman in the room was not
Diana, but Helena. Unable to tell

them apart in the dark, Bertram
promised to marry Diana and
said he would love her forever.

Helena started speaking to
him about love and how she too
wanted to marry him. It was a
pity that he would be leaving
tomorrow, as she was sure he
would forget about her in France.

But Bertram, hearing Diana reciprocate his feelings for the first time, promised that he would be back to ask for her hand in marriage. Now was the golden opportunity that Helena had been waiting for, and she asked Bertram to give her his ring to remind her of him, saying he would surely come back to reclaim it. Perhaps then, they could get married.

Bertram was so excited by the proposal that he handed Helena the ring, still thinking she was Diana. Helena in

turn handed him her own ring,
which in the darkness of the
night Bertram did not recognize.
Before morning, Helena sent
Bertram away. Then, along with
Diana and her mother, she set off
for Paris. There she learned that

the king had gone to visit her mother-in-law at her house in Rousillon. So Helena, with her entourage, made for Rousillon, close on the king's heels.

Meanwhile, the king had reached Rousillon and was talking tenderly to Bertram's mother about the late Helena, the girl who had cured him and whom her foolish son had rejected. Lafeu started weeping, remembering the sweet girl he had helped seek an audience with the king.

Just then, Bertram entered the room and the king noticed Helena's ring on his finger. This aroused his suspicions, as he remembered that Bertram had not been wearing it when he left France. He wondered if he had met Helena later and killed her, thereby acquiring the ring.

Diana and her mother entered the hall and entreated the king to marry Bertram to Diana, the girl he had promised to marry while in Florence. Diana went on to present the ring Bertram had given her during his last night in the Italian city. Bertram, scared that the king would severely punish him, immediately started to deny the whole affair. But the king was livid and ordered his guards to arrest both Bertram

and Diana, and hold them
until they told him the truth.

At that very moment, Helena
entered and revealed herself to
the people present. Bertram's
mother, the king, and Lafeu

were overjoyed to see her alive
and well. She explained how the
rings had been exchanged, and
everything that had happened
between them in Florence. She
then turned to Bertram and

showed him the letter, which said
that only if she could remove
the ring from his finger could
she call him her husband.

Bertram was surprised by
the love Helena felt for him. He
told her that if she could prove

it was her and not Diana whom he had spoken to that night, he would love her forever like he had never loved anyone before. This was soon proved by Diana and her mother, who explained the roles they had played.

The king was very pleased to hear of Diana's part and promised her that he would find her a noble husband as well. Bertram and Helena were now in love and

ready to live the rest of their
lives together. The king
could not help but remark,
"All's well that ends well!"